The Amazing Adventures
Of Freddie Whitemouse

A NOVEL

BOOKS FOR ADULTS BY
ELIZABETH JANE HOWARD

Love All
The Beautiful Visit
The Long View
The Sea Change
After Julius
Odd Girl Out
Something in Disguise
Getting It Right
Mr Wrong
Falling

The Cazalet Chronicles

The Light Years
Marking Time
Confusion
Casting Off
All Change

The Lover's Companion
Green Shades
Slipstream

The Amazing Adventures Of Freddie Whitemouse

A NOVEL

Elizabeth Jane Howard

ILLUSTRATIONS BY
BETHAN WOOLLVIN

MANTLE

First published 2016 by Mantle
an imprint of Pan Macmillan
20 New Wharf Road, London N1 9RR
Associated companies throughout the world
www.panmacmillan.com

ISBN 978-1-4472-9345-3

1 3 5 7 9 8 6 4 2

A CIP catalogue record for this book is available from the British Library.

Printed and bound by CPI Group (UK) Ltd, Croydon, CR0 4YY

Visit **www.panmacmillan.com** to read more about all our books
and to buy them. You will also find features, author interviews and
news of any author events, and you can sign up for e-newsletters
so that you're always first to hear about our new releases.

For my brother, Colin,
known as Monkey

In memoriam

Chapter One

*O*nce upon a time a very old white mouse had her seventy-fourth child – a small grey mouse she called Ulric because she had run out of names. He was born in a house called No. 3, The Grove, but his apartment in the house was No. 16, Skirting Board West. A great many other mouseholders lived there as well, but luckily several families of people also resided there, which meant that there was generally enough food to go round.

All of Mrs Whitemouse's children were born in a doll's summer hat, which was made of straw with a cherry-red ribbon and three daisies sewn to the brim. Mrs Whitemouse had made a good nest in the Hat out of chewed-up bus tickets and tiny bits of fluff that she found all over the place. When Ulric was very young he just stayed in the Hat, having drinks of milk and sleeping. Gradually he grew nice thick grey fur, and beautiful translucent ears – like your eyelids when you look into the sun – and a useful tail that tapered off to an elegant point. His eyes were shiny black like the buttons on a doll's boot and his whiskers were silvery white each side of his twisty nose – he could move it sideways as well as up and down. When he was nearly a full-grown mouse he announced that he wished to be called

Freddie. As he was known in the family for being rather moody, they all agreed to this.

The trouble was that Freddie really did not like being a mouse. 'It's just a phase,' his mother said at first, but it wasn't.

Weeks later, when Freddie was full grown, he was hating it more than ever. When he was younger he had been able to pretend that he would become eNORmouse – the size of one of the boots that people left in rows by the back door, the size of the bicycle that a man rode away on every morning, the size of the man himself . . . But after several weeks of not getting any larger than his mother, he was forced to recognise that he was a mouse, and a mouse he would remain. The thought horrified him. *I simply can't spend the rest of my life like this! If only someone would help me! Anyone!* He shut his charming beady eyes to squeeze the tears out, and when he opened them there was the most extraordinary creature squatting in front of him. He was so surprised (which is Mouse for frightened) that as he jumped backwards all he had time to notice was that the creature was about eight times his size and had two pitch-black unwinking eyes set at the edges of his wide flat head. 'Who are you?'

'I am a toad by birth and a sorcerer by profession. I heard your call for help, and here I am.' His very wide mouth got even wider, and Freddie's nose trembled in fear. The toad's mouth seemed to take up most of his body, and Freddie, who had been taught by his mother that quite a lot of creatures actually ate mice, was afraid that the toad might be one of those.

'What is it you want?' the sorcerer toad asked.

'I want to stop being a mouse.'

'Oh, that! No problem at all.'

'Good! And can you do it now? Change me, I mean?'

'I could, of course. Any idea what you want to change into?'

'Something larger. Actually, much larger.'

'Yes?'

'A tiger?'

He had heard of them from his mother, when his sister was complaining about the cat who prowled outside the house. 'Be grateful for small mercies,' his mother had said. 'If it was a tiger out there, none of us would stand a chance.'

The toad shook his head. 'You wouldn't like that. Either you'd live in a horrible hot jungle, or you'd be in a cage with people staring at you all day.'

Freddie suggested several more animals but the toad found objections to all of them. Monkeys were made to work in circuses, dogs were ignored by their owners and thrown out after Christmas, various birds were hunted.

Freddie felt very depressed. Then he had a good idea.

'Couldn't I just see what it would be like being a tiger, for instance – just for a couple of days? Then I could come back and report to you?'

There was silence while the toad dealt with a passing fly. His tongue shot out and the fly seemed to stick to it, and then, quick as lightning, both vanished and all Freddie could see was the light ripples of the skin on the underside of his chin.

'Where were we? Oh yes. Well, I'm afraid I'm not doing all that sorcery simply for a couple of days. A week is the least I'm prepared to offer. And even then, you will have to put up with retaining some of your murine characteristics.' Seeing that Freddie looked baffled, he added, 'Murine means mouselike; it is also your language. You speak Murine, and if I wasn't a sorcerer, I wouldn't understand a word you said. So, what is it to be? A tiger for a week, or a mere mouse for a lifetime?'

So Freddie chose (and I'm sure you would agree with him) to be a tiger for a week.

Chapter Two

Freddie must have been asleep, because the moment he opened an eye (the other one was squashed against something) he saw the most enormous paw just an inch or so away. It had huge, black, extremely sharp-looking claws at the end of it. *The end of me*, he thought in panic. Freddie was used – as most mice are – to being frightened, but this time there had been no warning – just an awful shock – like waking up to what you thought was a bad dream and it not being one. He could not move from fright.

But then the paw moved – stretched out past his head revealing a long furry limb . . . striped fur . . . He lifted his head and beyond the limb saw the body of a fully grown tiger who was now engaged in a slow, luxuriant stretch, which he found was most extraordinarily enjoyable. *It's me! I really am a tiger! Just what I wanted.*

He found he was lying on a ledge of a cliff that overlooked a small river and a few yards downstream he could see there was a pool with some animals drinking from it. He was surrounded by tall dry grass and the sun was very hot on his fur. Watching the creatures drinking made him feel thirsty and he decided to join them. There were large black birds, a number of greyish pigs with tusks . . . Best of all there was a herd of small deer; nervous drinkers – they would take a sip and then look up anxiously as though afraid of something. The sight of them brought a sudden rush of juices to his mouth. He had jumped off the ledge and now began to prowl through the long grass. Every time the deer stopped drinking, he crouched, motionless, until, reassured, they lowered their delicate noses to the water. A few more steps and he would be able to pounce . . .

But, oh dear! Just as he was about to make a grab for the deer he had picked out as being the nearest, a gang of monkeys burst out of the jungle, swinging down from the trees, rushing over the ground, whooping, chattering, even yelping. They saw Freddie at once and uttered such piercing shrieks of warning that all the deer immediately fled from the pool, along with the birds and the pigs. The monkeys crossed the river, leaping from rock to rock, and settled on the far side. Their cries subsided into a taunting gabble as they attacked some bushes that held small yellow fruits, spitting out the stones and watching him. Fruit was no good to him, he thought angrily, as he realised how very hungry he was.

Well, at least he could have a drink. He must have woken up very early in the morning, as it was now getting steadily hotter; the sky was bleached to a thick white – everything was breathlessly still except for the ticking and humming of tiny insects; the monkeys, having stripped the bushes, had gone as suddenly as they had arrived. Freddie's fur itched intolerably and all he wanted was to lie in the water, where it would be so much cooler than anywhere else. He waded cautiously in (as a mouse he had been afraid of water ever since he fell into a coffee cup that had been left outside No. 16, Skirting Board West; it had been full of thick black liquid and tasted horrible; various relatives had hauled him out by his tail) and soon found that he was out of his depth but it didn't matter because he was swimming! It was a lovely feeling; he swam across the pool and back several times until he almost began to feel cold. So he waded out and shook himself so that sparks of water shot out of his fur; the air was so hot that it seemed to dry him in minutes. But the swim had made him hungrier than ever, and as he padded off into the jungle the sudden thought of cheese overwhelmed him. You didn't have to hunt for cheese, it didn't run away from you when it saw you coming, it just lay there while you munched it up.

On the other hand, he realised wearily, jungles did not seem to have cheese in them. You needed people for cheese, and the jungle seemed pretty short of them. Perhaps I should explain here that if you are thinking of a jungle as a dense dark green place full of ferns and creepers and tall trees, you are thinking of rainforest, which is quite a different thing.

The jungle that Freddie found himself in was dry, because it hadn't rained for months, and was full of small shrubs and trees of varying sizes, with some open glades and a great deal of dry tall grass and sometimes large grey rocks. The glades, he discovered, were where the deer grazed: he came across two small herds of these, but they fled the moment he got near them. To begin with he chased them, but all that did was make him tired and even more in need of food.

But Freddie was not stupid. In a few hours he had learned to move soundlessly through the grass, to wait much longer before he started the chase, and, most important of all, that even when the deer did not see or hear him, they ran away if they smelled him, but if he got into a position where he could smell them it was much easier (hunters call this 'getting downwind', but Freddie didn't know that, never having met any). He certainly was not stupid, but all the unsuccessful chases had made him much weaker. *Next time*, he said to himself, *I've got to catch one. It might be my last chance.*

Eventually, in the early evening, he came across some deer who, though grazing, seemed also on the move, and he quickly guessed that they were making their way to the drinking place at the river. So he went ahead of them and chose a really good position beside some rocks only a few yards from where the deer would have to come. His striped fur blended in with the tall yellowy grass, so well that you or I would never have known he was there unless we happened to catch sight of his stern yellow eyes that were fixed upon the single point where, because of the rocks opposite, the deer would have to come in a single file to reach the pool. He could hear them coming now, their feet making small crackling noises in the dry undergrowth. He let three go past him and then he sprang.

He went straight for his victim's throat, and almost before he brought the deer down, it stopped struggling and the others all fled. He dragged his prey to a shady spot under a tree and settled down to a feast. His sharp claws and his very rough tongue meant that he could get at all the bits he found that as a tiger he liked most. He purred as he ate (he had the most enormous purr that sounded almost like an engine). After an hour of feasting he could eat no more, so he dragged the remains of the carcass to a place between two rocks. He was full to the brim of deer and extremely sleepy. He climbed onto the lowest branch of a tree, draped himself gracefully along it and fell into a deep, contented sleep.

He woke suddenly; it was a starless night, the sky was as dark and dense as black velvet and the moon was veiled in cloud. What woke him was the sounds that seemed to be coming from the rocks where he had hidden the remains of his kill. Someone had found it – it sounded like more than one someone – and was making a series of high-pitched growls, punctuated by little yelps. As Freddie began to lower himself out of the tree he was beset by two conflicting thoughts: the first, how dare anyone try to steal his food; the second, ah! perhaps he would at last have some company – something that had been worrying him ever since he had arrived in the jungle, but that had been ignored because of his more urgent need for water and food. He was used to living with company – not only immediate relations like his brothers and sisters, but quantities of cousins and friends. He remembered a time when a human inhabitant of 3, The Grove had dropped a packet of cornflakes there had been an all-night party and how they had made so much noise that Mrs Whitemouse had given them a lecture the next morning on how there would be traps with cheese in them 'and you will die like your poor Uncle Herbert'.

Freddie prowled carefully towards the rocks, and when he had nearly reached them the moon suddenly came out. Two quite small animals – he could tell they were not tigers because they had plain black fur instead of stripes – were tearing pieces of meat off his deer – not only stealing from him, but stealing from each other, with growls and slashing of claws. Their faces and paws were streaked with blood, and they were play-fighting in between eating. He was just about to say, 'That's enough, you two,' (they were only cubs, after all – far smaller than he was) when a low, distinctly ominous snarl stopped him. Out of the shadows of the rocks – invisible until she moved – came a full-grown jaguar. Her tail was twitching and her yellow eyes were fixed upon Freddie as she continued to snarl, baring her long, pointed teeth as she edged her way around the carcass until she was between him and her cubs. The message was clear; if he made any move towards them, she would attack: the fact that he was larger than she made no difference to her.

The cubs had stopped their antics and their mother must have said something to them, because they left the carcass and ran away into the long grass. How long he and the jaguar mother stood staring at one another Freddie did not know, but just when he was wondering what he should do, a small cloud raced in front of the moon, and when it had cleared, the mother had vanished. When he was quite sure that she had gone, Freddie inspected what was left of his kill.

Precious little; a rather mangled haunch – bits of hoof and fur and dried blood, much of it smelling strongly of jaguar. Partly because of this, and partly because he was full anyway, Freddie didn't fancy eating any more. Sadness overwhelmed him. *I would have allowed her to have some of my deer if only she had been more friendly,* he thought. He was simply longing to have someone to talk to, and so far all the animals he had encountered had either fled in terror, or, in the case of the jaguar, had made it clear that they were quite prepared to hurt him. *She didn't give me a chance to say that I wouldn't have harmed her cubs,* he thought, but then (and this was because Freddie was at heart an unusually honest tiger) he had to admit that if he had been as hungry as he'd been before he caught the deer, he probably would have killed them. *If I could only meet another tiger* . . . he thought – rather hopelessly – he had an uncomfortable feeling that tigers did not go in for the easy-going social life he had been used to as a mouse.

Freddie's mother had only to go out for afternoon crumbs and a few weeks later there would be a whole load of new arrivals in the Hat, and another uncle added to the family. He could see now that if tigers behaved like that the whole jungle would be littered with them and there would very soon be a severe shortage of food. Still, he could not help wishing that this bit of jungle was a bit littered – a nice female tigress that could look after him as his mother had . . . But here his imagination failed him. He distracted himself with a thorough clean-up of his claws which still had awkward bits of deer in them.

'Better start hunting before I actually need another meal,' he said to himself (there was no one else to say it to). It was early morning, but it was already getting hot.

For the next two days he hunted for deer, stalked them at every possible opportunity and failed to catch anything. He went back to the pool twice for water. The small river had been reduced to a mere trickle, but he followed its course upstream in search of another pool. Then, late in the afternoon on the second day, he found one – larger than the first. It was surrounded by rocks, but it had one corner where it was quite shallow, with a sandy beach that was richly imprinted with the feet of many animals. He was so hot and tired that he decided to have a swim before he worked out a plan of attack. Evening, he knew, was when deer came down to drink.

The moment he was in the water, an idea came to him. If he stayed there, motionless, with just his nose out of the water, the deer would not notice him until it was too late. He waited . . .

But – oh dear! There was at first a vague rumbling sound – a crashing sort of noise, as if branches were being pulled off trees – and then a herd of elephants appeared. It was not a big herd – more like a family, one gigantic, three smaller, and one very perky baby who kept trotting in and out of the others' way as they trod ponderously towards the water.

Freddie was terrified. With their huge ears flapping, their enormous trunks swaying and their curving pointed tusks, they loomed steadily nearer and nearer until all he could see was elephant. Just as he made up his mind to make a dash for the shore, the father elephant made a very loud shrieking sound, twice: his family all stood still while he walked ahead of them into the pool towards Freddie.

It was now or never. 'When in doubt, run,' his mother had repeatedly said to him when he was young and inclined to show off about the horrible cat who lived in The Grove. Well, he wasn't in doubt now; he had to run for his life. He started to swim away from the huge elephant, who was so close that Freddie could see his small angry eyes. Then, as the elephant paused, Freddie doubled back around the creature and the moment he was back in his depth, he sprang from the water and dashed past the family and away into the long grass. His fur was all bedraggled and he was panting for breath.

When he felt at a safe distance from the elephants he started searching for a quiet place where he could rest until his fur was dry. He found what looked like a good place – a pile of rocks around a small cave with a sandy sunlit patch at its entrance, which was so narrow that he had to squeeze to get his head and shoulders in.

It was not entirely dark inside because there was a cleft in the rocks that formed the roof, but almost before he had noticed this there was a low, most ominous hissing noise, and in the patchy gloom there reared a large and long black snake who seemed to be wearing a hood. Her head was swaying, but her eyes – like very shiny little black berries – were fixed upon him. As she glided nearer he could see a pile of small creamy-coloured eggs that were placed exactly where the sun came through the roof. He did not know that she was a cobra, but he knew at once that the eggs were hers and he knew what mothers were like if they thought that their children were in any sort of danger. He was out of that cave before you could say Freddie Whitemouse.

For a long time he padded through the jungle. He felt sad as well as hungry. He even got to thinking rather longingly of a delicious bacon rind he had discovered near a dustbin once, and how his mother had made him share it with a crowd of brothers and sisters. 'You must learn to think of others,' she had scolded. Here there were no others to think of, but on the other hand there wasn't a bacon rind in sight. *Anyway, I'd need about a hundred bacon rinds to fill me up.* This made him realise that he wouldn't like them anyway.

All day he had been following the riverbed, which was mostly dried up, until suddenly it was joined by a stream that trickled in over some rocks. He stopped, because he could hear the sounds of people ahead. All his life he had been aware that people were dangerous – certainly to mice, and most probably, he thought, to tigers. He had reached the top of a grassy slope and craned his neck to get a better view. Part of the jungle had been cleared of shrubs and long grass and there was a cluster of little huts; people were digging earth, and a woman in a bright pink dress was walking from the river carrying a large pot on her head. Freddie was looking so hard at all this that he didn't notice what was happening behind him until two boys driving some goats towards the village saw him, and shouted and ran down the hill waving sticks at the goats, who scrambled ahead of them. But the youngest goat got left behind. It froze for only a second or two, bleating for its mother, but those seconds were enough for Freddie. He hurled himself through the air and a moment later the kid was dead and he was dragging it away from the village back into thicker jungle.

It was only a baby goat, and he ate everything except the hoofs and the horns, which were tiny. (If you feel that this was cruel of Freddie, you have to remember that tigers kill their prey in seconds by suffocating them; a small goat is for them the equivalent of you having sausages and eggs, and he was – as most tigers are when they kill – terrifically hungry.)

Anyway, when he had finished he felt too full and sleepy to search for a suitable tree, so he settled down on a narrow ledge of rock over-looking the dry riverbed. He licked his paws and face clean of goat and stretched himself out so that he completely filled up the ledge with only his tail hanging down, shut his yellow eyes and slept.

. . . He was back at No. 3, The Grove. How amazed they would all be when they saw him! How they would admire his magnificent stripy coat, his long rich tail, and how he would frighten the terrible cat that was always trying to catch any member of his family who came her way! The back door of the house was ajar and he pushed it open with his mighty paw, but alas! When he reached No. 16, Skirting Board West, with its tiny little entrance, of course he couldn't possibly get in. He got down on the floor and put his eye to the hole, and there was his mother standing on her hind legs staring at his large yellow eye. 'It's me – Freddie,' he began to say. He thought he was talking quietly, but quiet for a tiger is loud to a mouse, and Mrs Whitemouse gave one squeak of terror and fainted. There was a lot of squeaking and gibbering from the family, but all he could see was a bit of his mother's pale pinky stomach that had hardly any fur on it trembling with terror. Then she was being helped away from the entrance hole, and then he couldn't see anything, because the hole was blocked up by what he recognised as a dog biscuit. They did not want him – his own family; he would have to live the rest of his life without any of them . . . Just as black despair rolled over him like a dark and terrifying fog, he woke.

You know that feeling when you wake up after a bad dream? A part of you feels awfully glad to be back in your life, safe and warm in your own bed, but also, to begin with, the dream felt so real that you still feel frightened, until gradually it slips away into the smallest corner of your mind, where it becomes 'only a dream'. Well, Freddie felt like that, but slowly the heat on his fur, and the tiny ticking noises of the jungle around him, and particularly the flies that kept maddeningly trying to get into his eyes, brought him back to the present – he was one thirsty tiger, and the nearest water was the pool where there were people.

He made himself wait until dusk before he padded quietly down to the pool. All was silent, no sign of deer, but although there was no sign of people either, he could smell a smoky, spicy odour – a smell of cooking, which he knew was what people did with their food before they ate it (No. 3, The Grove was often full of cooking smells). There was also the distant but enticing scent of goats, and he decided that the next meal he would have would be one of them again. He would have to wait until those boys took the goats out to find food for them to eat. After a quick uneasy drink, (he had the uncomfortable feeling that he was being watched) he spent much of the night prowling about trying to find a good place to ambush the goats.

All the following hot, thirsty day he waited and waited, but there was no sign of goats or boys. He was hungry again – the next goat he caught would have to be a larger one.

Two more days and nights went by, and although when Freddie went to the pool in the evenings he could smell goat, he didn't see one. By now he was famished – starving, he felt – and he could think of nothing but food.

On the third morning, he went – very early – back to the grassy slope where he had seen the village. This time he noticed that there was a track where the boys had herded the goats. It was quite narrow and on each side of it there was the usual long dry grass and a few trees. It was not straight, so when he started to follow it he could not see ahead further than the next bend. He padded cautiously down it, ready to leap aside and take cover if any people appeared. The scent of the goats got stronger and stronger as he descended, and his excitement and hunger were so intense that he was trembling as he became sure that any moment now he would at last find his next meal. Then, suddenly, the path or track divided into two paths, and just as he was trying to choose between them he was struck by a really strong odour of raw meat. It came from the left-hand path, so he started along it.

Then he saw it. A large piece of goat was hanging from a low branch of a tree ahead. Blood was dripping from it. All ideas of caution vanished. The branch was only about five feet from the ground and he sprang towards it. Plonk! Before he could grab the haunch, the ground gave way under him and he fell heavily into a deep hole.

For a moment he lay stunned. His right shoulder was hurting and he saw that it had been pierced by a sharp stick that was still embedded in his fur. The shock and pain made him snarl. He tried to get to his feet – the pit, though deep, was so narrow and small that there was hardly space for him, but in any case his shoulder had become a stabbing pain. If he was to escape, he must pull the stick out. So he gripped it with his front teeth and, growling in agony, he tugged until it suddenly came loose. The wound started to bleed, but gradually he licked it clean.

Escape! He must get out of this awful hole. His eyes were getting accustomed to the gloom and a small amount of light came from the top where he had fallen through. But he could now see that the sides of the pit were studded with sticks like the one that had wounded him. There was no room for him to spring out, and if he tried to claw up the sides the sticks would stab him. It was a trap, he realised. The boys had made a trap and put the piece of goat on the branch to get him to fall into it. If he was to escape, he would have to wait until the people came to get him out. Then a really awful thought came to him. Supposing they did not come? Supposing they just left him to die of hunger and thirst? And how could they get him out anyway? He was so cramped that there was hardly room for him to stand. He tried to be angry and not frightened; when they came he'd go for them – he'd teach them not to mess about with tigers – he'd wrap his mighty paw around one of their necks . . . but then a fresh wave of terror overcame him; he could feel his heart thumping and he was trembling with fear. He let out one despairing roar – a kind of growling groan – the loudest noise he had ever made in his life. It somehow made him feel a little bit better, so he did it again – twice more.

He could hear the people coming; several of them, he did not know how many. They were jabbering away. When he looked up, he could see one of them peering down at him. He kept up a low growl, but there was not even room for him to lash his tail. Eventually one of them climbed a little way down into the pit – staying well out of Freddie's reach – and then, once the man had stopped climbing, Freddie felt a sudden piercing pain in his shoulder – the one that hadn't been stabbed by the stick – and he snarled with the shock. The pain wasn't like the stick had been; in fact, this one didn't go on hurting. He stood for a moment; he felt very unsteady – tired – so tired he wasn't even frightened, he just wanted . . . and as he tried to think of what he wanted, he collapsed in a furry heap.

Chapter Three

'Wake up! Your week is up! None too soon, by the look of you.'

There was no mistaking the croaky voice, and when he managed to open his eyes (he felt very groggy), there were the two black eyes very wide apart in the flat head looking down at him. Freddie felt extremely weak, and one of his shoulders ached: the sorcerer was so much larger than he was, that he realised he was no longer a tiger, but back to being himself – Freddie Whitemouse. The relief was enormous. There was a brief silence while he was fixed with an unblinking gaze.

'Well?'

'Well, what?'

'How did it go – being a tiger?'

'Not too bad.' He was determined to put a brave face on his extraordinary week, and that cost him much effort, as it is difficult for a mouse to put a brave face on anything.

The toad's already amazingly wide mouth seemed to get momentarily wider; if he was smiling, it was rather a sarcastic smile. 'Perhaps you would like to go back to it then?'

'No, thank you.'

'Well, at least you escaped being in a cage in a zoo for the rest of your life.'

'Is that what was going to happen?'

'Certainly. Those men who trapped you know

that they get far much more money for a live tiger than a dead one. You would have ended up in a very small cage with a lot of people staring at you and telling each other you were a tiger. If you ask me, you've been pretty lucky for a mouse.'

'I suppose I have.' He did not feel in the least lucky: his shoulder was throbbing and he felt weak with hunger. 'I didn't actually ask you,' he said after a moment.

'Ask me what?'

'Whether I was lucky.'

'No. Well, gratitude is not your strong point.' He paused to deal with a passing fly. 'In fact,' he said after thinking about it, 'it is quite difficult to think what your strong points are.'

Freddie thought – or tried to think.

'Brave? I think I'm quite brave about most things.'

'Poo! Tigers don't have much to be brave about.'

'But mice have to be brave about nearly everything. I've had quite a lot of practice, and compared to the rest of my family I am regarded as having the most courage. I *am* brave,' he finished defiantly, but his voice was all squeaky and shaky from having been so frightened and hungry for so long.

There was a pause, and then the sorcerer – in a much kinder voice – said, 'I was saving this bluebottle for my lunch, but you can have it if you like – I can see you need sustenance.'

Freddie looked at the uninviting sight of the fat dead bluebottle.

'I don't need sust— whatever you said; it's food I really need. I'm so hungry I could eat a dog biscuit.' This was a saying well known in his family, because Mrs Whitemouse insisted upon keeping a very old pink dog biscuit in the home, 'In case,' she frequently said, 'of an emergency.' So far they had never had one, and most of the younger mice had no idea what she even meant. It was the biscuit that had blocked up the front door in Freddie's dream. As he remembered this, a wave of homesickness overcame him; his beady eyes glittered with tears, but he was determined not to cry in front of the toad, so he swallowed several times and thought hard about his reputation for braveness.

'I think I'd like to go home and think things over before I try the next thing.'

'All right. But you can only have two days if you do want another go. I'm not prepared to hang about waiting to use up my sorcery on you whenever you happen to feel like it. Two days, and then either you meet me by the water tank in the greenhouse, or you stay a mouse forever.'

'I don't want to do that.'

'Suit yourself. And next time you are offered a treat, you should thank the person who offers it, whether you want it or not.'

And then, as Freddie nodded obediently, the toad added, 'It's called gratitude. Or simply good manners. Take your pick.' And he turned his immensely broad back on Freddie and at the same time disappeared.

Freddie looked around and realised that he was in the back garden of No. 3, The Grove, outside the battered old greenhouse with its panes of broken glass and rotting woodwork. Home was only minutes away, or at least it would have been only minutes if he had been up to running, but his shoulder hurt and he felt so weak and tired that he was practically crawling and had to keep stopping to rest. Luckily there was a way in through the back of the house. 'Never mind,' he said to himself; he would be going back to a hero's welcome; his mother would give him a delicious supper and then, with any luck, he would go to sleep in the Hat.

But it didn't turn out at all like that. His mother was pleased to see him, but she was also cross with him for disappearing for a week without telling her, and her crossness somehow spoiled the pleased bit. I don't know whether you have noticed this about some grown-ups: they will ask you quite boring questions like 'Did you have a good day at school?' but when you tell them something really fascinating, they don't seem at all interested. She did give Freddie a nice meal –

some cornflakes, two sultanas, a walnut and a strand of macaroni that had delicious flakes of cheese in it – but when he started to tell her about being a tiger, she simply said things like, 'Yes, dear,' and, 'Well, I never!' and, 'Really, Freddie! I don't know where you get it all from.'

His younger relations, however, were absolutely riveted. They sat in a circle around him and wanted to know every single detail – about the jungle and the other animals and how he had got food to eat. When he told them about the jaguars and elephants, they trembled and squeaked with excitement and fright and frequently said how brave he must have been. He was a hero to them.

He was just about to tell them about the cobra when Mrs Whitemouse interrupted. 'That's enough of all that nonsense. If you go frightening the young ones with your silly stories, they won't sleep a wink.' And she sent them all to bed, and no, he could not sleep in the Hat, because it was full of the new babies. He did not mind this too much, because several of the older mice had quite a quarrel about who should sleep next to him. But one of his youngest sisters did have a nightmare, and woke up squeaking with terror; 'Freddie! Freddie! Save me!' and not until she was safely squeezed against his chest and everybody else was awake did he find out that she thought a tiger was going to eat her up entirely. 'You said eating a mouse for a tiger would be like us eating a cake crumb! I don't want to be a crumb!' she wept. Freddie told her again and again that tigers did not eat mice, but she got to sleep next to him, which he suspected was why she had had the bad dream in the first place.

The next day there was hardly any breakfast. The mice who were supposed to have been foraging during the night had practically all stayed at home listening to Freddie, and one of his uncles – who never did a stroke of work – now went on and on about team spirit, but the few mice who had gone foraging did not seem inclined to share their food. *Not much team spirit there*, Freddie thought. He was hungry and felt that if he was such a hero, he should be one of the first to be fed.

So – feeling rather sulky, but brave; after all, he had become used to hunting for his meals during the last week – he went out in broad daylight to have a look around the dustbins in the front garden of No. 3, The Grove.

He was lucky. One of the bins had overflowed and he found the remains of a ham sandwich – the crust and a small sliver of ham – and an open and almost empty tin of dog food (he knew from the smell that it was dog food because Mrs Whitemouse had once brought some back from the bowl in the kitchen when some of the people had gone out for a walk with their dog). He had to get into the tin to eat it, but it was absolutely delicious. By the time he emerged from the tin, he was completely full (in fact he felt rather sick) so he found a nice dark place under the garden hedge where he could clean his sticky whiskers and fur. He no longer wanted the sandwich so he decided to leave it. It would be madness to try to drag it back in daylight. He had a little refreshing sleep before returning to his crowded and noisy home.

And it *was* noisy – and crowded. There simply wasn't enough room for the whole family.

His mother was reproachful and distracted. 'Where have you been? Your brothers have been working all morning on the new apartments in Skirting Board East: they were counting on you to help them.' She was cleaning some very new tiny mice in the Hat and trying to make some of the older ones share two apple peelings, and they were all protesting 'I found them! . . . I dragged one of them back here . . . She didn't do anything, so why should she have any of them?' But when they caught sight of Freddie, they dropped the apple peel and rushed over to him crying, 'Tell us a story; Freddie, please, please, tell us another story. The one about the wicked snake you started last night!'

'I'll only tell it if you do as Mother says about the apple peel.' And they did. They gnawed the peel into twenty pieces without eating any of them, and then crouched quietly around Freddie: twenty pairs of beady eyes fixed on his face, twenty sets of whiskers twitching with excitement.

Mrs Whitemouse looked over the brim of the Hat, shrugged and said, 'Anything to keep them quiet, but none of that tiger nonsense – it's time you stopped showing off.' This made Freddie feel that his mother did not love him, and he felt very sad.

However, he did his best. Instead of saying he was the tiger he simply said, 'Once there was a tiger . . .'

But it was no good. The story sounded somehow dull – he could see they didn't believe in it. 'But you were the tiger, weren't you, Freddie? It all happened to you, didn't it?'

And one very small sister called Violet said, 'What happened is that you got magicked into a tiger – that's what.' And there was a chorus of agreement.

Freddie stared in amazement, but before he

could say anything, one of the older boys said, 'Don't be silly, Violet. What do you know about magic anyway?'

'Someone called Alberto told me. He did tricks with bird seed: they were conjuring tricks, so I do know.'

'And who is this wonderful Alberto?'

'He lives in apartment No. 72 East. I see him sometimes.' Freddie noticed that her pale pink nose had suddenly become much pinker. 'Tell us about the wicked snake, Freddie. Did it try to bite you to death?'

'Don't be silly, Violet. A snake couldn't kill a tiger.'

'Oh, do shut up, Eustace. Let Uncle Freddie get on with the story.' And Violet insisted, 'And you are the tiger, Freddie. I just know you are.' Her bright beseeching eyes were too much for him. He would go back to being the tiger, which, after all, was true. But when it came to the snake part of his tale, he did not want to tell of his uncourageous retreat, and so he made it a braver story. 'It came nearer and nearer, rearing up and making its black head wide – like a great hood – and hissing horribly. But I stood my ground. I said, "If you come any nearer, I will smite you with my mighty paw, and you will be dead and your eggs will have nobody to look after them when your children come out of them." And the snake went back into the cave to her eggs.'

'And then what?'

'I left her. In peace.'

'Did each of the eggs have a wicked snake inside?'

'Of course.'

'Didn't you wait to see them all come out?'

'I had more important things to do.'

'Oh, Freddie, you are so brave!'

There was a chorus of agreement.

Freddie's mother interrupted. 'Time for your suppers and bed.' To Freddie, she said, 'Well, at least you kept them quiet with your nonsense.'

A moment later she added, 'It's dark enough

now; you'd better join your cousins foraging – do something useful for a change.'

Freddie simply could not understand why she was being so horrible to him. He looked around the dim den, crowded as usual and enlivened with the sound of twenty mice chewing apple peel, and made off down the main mouse-made passage that ended in the kitchen of one of the apartments in the building. The people who lived in the ground-floor flat were not at all tidy and did not do very much cleaning. This was an ideal situation for Freddie's family. Things got dropped on the floor, left on the table, kept in flimsy paper bags that were easy to chew through. Plates were seldom washed up, and often contained delicious snacks like scrambled egg, bacon rind, sometimes even bits of toast with melted cheese on them. Cornflakes and crumbs were all over the place. The only danger was that the people who lived there often turned up to make themselves something to eat. Then the foragers had to hide and keep very quiet until the person or people had gone. Luckily the people hated cats, and the horrible cat from next door had stopped trying to get in after he had been drenched by a boy with a water pistol. Freddie's Uncle Herbert, who had seen this, said he laughed so much that even his whiskers ached, and he told the story so often that the family got bored of it. *And they'll get bored of my stories as well*, he thought. It was the custom for the foragers to eat on the spot before they carted stuff home for the others. Freddie wasn't very hungry after his huge morning meal, but he nibbled on some cake crumbs while he watched his cousin Horatio, a rather bossy athletic mouse who had managed to get onto the kitchen table, where he had found a half-eaten packet of crisps and a saucer with some peanuts. These he was pushing one by one over the edge of the table, ordering each of the others to take one of them home. Some of the peanuts had split and this made them easy to carry by mouth, but the whole ones were too big and had to be rolled along the floor. Freddie noticed a rather shy mouse trying to take a whole nut in her mouth. Horatio was shouting at her. She was shaking with fright and then suddenly the nut split in two. 'Now look what you've done!' Horatio roared. She burst into tears.

Freddie flew to her aid. 'Shut up, you bully!' he squeaked with rage. 'Nuts do split. It wasn't your fault,' he said to the poor mouse. 'Please cheer up.' He really couldn't bear to see her crying. He offered his tail to mop her tears and she accepted; he noticed that the round tops of her ears and her nose had gone a much darker pink.

'We could each take half the nut,' he said, and she nodded gratefully.

They left the kitchen with Horatio still shouting orders at the last few unfortunate mice in the foraging party.

The tunnel back to Freddie's home was too narrow for two mice so they had to go in single file. Freddie led the way.

'Why, if it isn't Lavinia!' exclaimed his mother

when they emerged in the den. 'How are you, my dear? And how is your dear aunt?'

His mother was sorting out the booty brought back by the foragers, while the little mice crouched in a ring around her waiting for their supper.

'She hasn't been very well, Mrs Whitemouse, so she sent me to get some supper. Freddie has been helping me. He saved me from Horatio.'

'I'm glad to hear it. That mouse will come to no good – frightening all the young ones out of their wits. Stay and have your supper with us, and I'll find something nice for you to take home to your aunt and then Freddie will see you safely home.'

So that is what happened. Lavinia led the way, and Freddie, armed with a delicious potato crisp, followed. When they reached the passage to Lavinia's home (which turned out to be No. 16, Skirting Board East), she turned to Freddie and said, 'I can manage perfectly well from here. Thank you so much for everything.'

'Wouldn't you like me to take the supper into your home for you?'

Lavinia looked suddenly frightened. 'Oh no. You see, my aunt wouldn't like it. She might think you were . . .' She stopped, her nose and her ears blushing again. 'She doesn't like me bringing friends home. Not like your mother at all. She is so kind to everyone, isn't she?

'But thank you,' she called as she disappeared down the passageway.

Kind to everyone except me, Freddie thought dismally as he ran home.

But when he got back, his mother seemed in a good mood. The tiny mice were huddled together asleep in the Hat, and the slightly older mice were lying in neat rows; Mrs Whitemouse had counted them to make sure they were all there, and they were. There was just space beside the Hat for her and Freddie.

'Lavinia is a very nice, well-behaved mouse.' She was whispering. 'And ever since her aunt had that nasty accident, she has had to look after her.'

'What nasty accident?'

'She was caught by that horrible cat, who kept

letting her go and then catching her again. One of her legs got broken. The dog chased the cat away, and Lavinia's poor aunt crawled home. But she hasn't been in her right mind since. She won't ever go out, and she won't see any of us – only Lavinia.' There was a pause, and then she added (mysteriously to Freddie), 'You could do a lot worse.' She gave him an affectionate nudge with her nose and fell instantly asleep.

He spent some time wondering what she meant, but was mainly just glad that she was being friendly again.

He never knew afterwards whether he had had a dream about it, or whether it was some flash of inspiration, but he woke up the next day quite certain that he would go to the sorcerer and ask to be a dog. Possibly it was his mother's story about the dog saving Lavinia's aunt from the cat; certainly his time in the dog-food tin had something to do with it. Dogs did not have to hunt and struggle for food. They got fed from special bowls every day. They got taken about in cars, went for walks, even had games with balls and suchlike. They got stroked a lot, and their owners kept telling them how good and beautiful they were. Put like that, it seemed a pretty good life.

They spent hours asleep in special beds their owners got for them. A dog's life was the thing.

This idea became clearer and more urgent throughout the following day (his last before meeting the sorcerer). He spent it slaving away at enlarging the Whitemouse home – which meant chewing away at floors and skirting boards and trying to get the younger mice to cart the chewed bits outside. It was a crowded, noisy and exhausting day, at the end of which he was expected to go foraging again. He went to see if the bit of ham sandwich was still by the dustbins, but it wasn't. On top of all this labour the younger mice were clamouring for a story while they had their supper. By then he was so worn out that he simply wanted a bit of peace and quiet. When he said he'd told them all his stories they simply said, 'Tell us again. Tell us about the jaguars; tell us about the elephants – no, tell us about the snake.' The snake was their favourite. Mrs Whitemouse shrugged and said on his own shoulders be it, which he didn't understand at all, but felt that in some way she was blaming him. He told the story, noticing that the cobra, from being about five feet long two days ago, was now nearer fifteen. It didn't matter; they squeaked with joyful terror, which was what they wanted.

Being a hero was actually rather tiring, he thought, as he settled down for the night – his last, possibly, as a mouse. He quenched the tremor of fear at this thought; he must be trembling with excitement – he was well known for his courage so naturally he was not in the least afraid.

Chapter Four

'And what may I do for you this morning?'

The sorcerer had ingeniously placed himself against a corner of the water tank in the greenhouse where at odd intervals a tap dripped one huge, reluctant drop onto the top of his head. Then he would look up and the drop would dribble slowly down his back to add to the shallow puddle in which he crouched. He had breakfasted off twenty-eight mosquitoes, and was in a contented frame of mind.

'I've decided that I want to be a dog.'

'What kind of dog?'

'Er – a large dog.' After a pause during which the toad eyed him unblinkingly, he added, 'And beautiful – by dog standards, that is. So that everyone will love me.'

'You've considered the drawbacks, of course.'

'Not really, because I don't know what they are. But I've thought a lot about the advantages – the good side.'

'And what do you consider them to be?'

'Well, dogs don't have to hunt for food . . .' He listed all the advantages that had occurred to him when he'd first had the idea, ending with being loved by everyone.

The toad listened. It was impossible to tell from his expression what he was thinking. Then he said, 'Of course I can turn you into a dog – even a specific breed of dog – but after that the life you lead will be entirely a matter of chance; it's nothing to do with me. Nor,' he added ominously, 'might it have very much, if anything, to do with you.'

There was a silence during which Freddie heard a monstrous drop of water plop onto the toad's head. He felt confused. What did the toad mean – things not having very much, if anything, to do with him?

While he was puzzling about that, the toad interrupted: 'Before we go any further, I have two statements to make.' He cleared his throat in a rich, croaky manner. 'One: this is the last time I'm prepared to do any sorcery for you. Officially I retired last year. It was merely because I hadn't switched off my magic properly that I heard from you – messages occasionally still got through. Also, I have to admit that I was a trifle bored. People usually wish to be more of whatever they are in the first place, and your desire to be someone completely different intrigued me. So – you have just one more chance. Two: the same rules apply as they did when you became a tiger. You will have precisely one week as whoever you choose to be. You then come back to me and decide whether you wish to remain a dog or whatever animal or go back to being a mouse. And that will be all. Is that clear?'

Freddie nodded. He was feeling more and more nervous and could not prevent his nose from twitching quite violently.

'Could you choose the kind of dog for me? I'm afraid I don't know any of their names.'

The sorcerer looked at him consideringly. 'Let me see: large, beautiful and everyone loving you – poodles, red setters, Afghans . . . Ah! I've got it! A lurcher! That's the best one for you. But before we agree on that, I feel I should warn you that this time you will not remember anything at all about being a mouse. You will be entirely a dog, and nothing but a dog. Understood?'

Freddie, reminding himself that he was a hero

and extremely brave, nodded again – he was trembling too much to speak.

The sorcerer said some words that Freddie could not understand, and then his voice got so faint that it didn't matter, because everything somehow faded into dark rushing air – and then stopped.

Chapter Five

'Charley! Up!'

He got slowly out of his basket, stretching his long back legs luxuriously and wagging his tail. Poppy called him like that every morning. Now she was sitting up in her bed, holding out her small thin arms and calling, 'Come on, Charley. Good boy – you know you can do it.'

Every morning he pretended to her that he couldn't make it – went through one or two false starts before he leapt, with graceful ease, onto the bed and stood over her with his front paws each side of her shoulders while he cleaned her face in an ecstasy of affection. She screwed up her eyes and tried to push his face away, but not very hard, and he knew she did not mean it. She smelled sweetly of biscuits she called digestives; whenever they were on the tea table, she secretly gave him delicious morsels. It was her morning smell, and it didn't seem to have much to do with whether she'd been eating them or not. Smells, he decided, were his favourite thing, which was just as well because his life was absolutely full of them. Of course some were awful: Poppy's father smelled of the cigars that he smoked, and – worse – of some drink he drank a lot, but out of faithfulness to Poppy Charley submitted to his rather sporting pats and having his ears carelessly pulled.

He had made his way under the duvet, and now lay with his head on her shoulder, his bony back pressed against her side and his arms and hind legs stretched stiffly out. Poppy put an arm around his neck; 'Oh, Charley, I do love you such an enormous amount. I wish I had coffee-coloured fur like you, and lovely glowing eyes and a beautiful friendly tail!'

He was unable to tell her that he loved her just as she was, but his tail thumped and he gave a deep sentimental sigh and hoped that she understood. Soon, he knew, the person who was not Poppy's mother – as she didn't seem to have one – would come hurrying in, ordering Poppy to get dressed for breakfast (people had far more meals than dogs). For weeks and weeks Poppy had had to go to school for most of the day; the woman – Poppy's father called her the house-keeper – would walk with her to the bus stop. Once he had followed them, and when Poppy got on the bus he sprang onto it as well and there was an awful fuss; the housekeeper dragged him off and scolded him and tied her scarf to his collar and was horrible to him all the way home.

Anyway while Poppy was out at school he slept a lot in his basket on the blanket she had knitted for him, but he always woke at five minutes to four because he knew she was nearly home. She would have tea while he sat beside her getting discreet pieces of cake or biscuit, which he swallowed with equal discretion.

Then they would go for a walk – or in his case a run. Where they lived was not really country, but their house was on the edge of a very large park where there were deer, and people went riding. Sometimes Poppy rode a pony, who always wanted to kick him, and he enjoyed bounding around him, always just out of reach. On fine days they would go to Poppy's favourite tree, a very large old oak whose lower branches made for easy climbing, and he would sit guarding her. Sometimes she would bring a ball, which she would throw for him to retrieve. No matter how many times he slogged back with it, she would throw the ball again. He couldn't see the point of it himself, but she seemed to enjoy it. He really didn't mind what they did as long as they were together. Naturally they liked some different things: she didn't share his deep interest in lamp posts, railings, street corners, and other dogs' bottoms, for instance, and he couldn't see the point of books at all. Years ago, he dimly remembered, he had tried chewing one, but he hadn't enjoyed it: Mrs Keeper had hit him with a slipper and – much worse – Poppy had cried, so never again. They had a very different approach to people; when he had met someone once, he could forever afterwards tell who they were from a mile off, but Poppy always had to see them close up and would touch them, or talk about what they looked like. She did once (and he would never forget it) say that she loved the smell of his warm fur – the best thing that anyone had ever said to him.

This particular morning, which was Freddie's first day of being a dog called Charley, was full of feelings that didn't seem to go with one another. On the one hand it was a morning like any other of the countless mornings when he had woken up with Poppy calling him; on the other hand he kept feeling that something quite different was going to start happening at any moment – something new and awful.

He wanted to warn Poppy, but how can you warn someone if you don't speak their language, and anyway you don't know what you are warning them about? All he could do was stick close to her. He had to have his morning potter in the garden, but he practised his guarding growl, and by the time Poppy was having her breakfast he was sitting watchfully beside her.

There seemed to be a lot of commotion in the house; people he didn't know kept tramping up and down the stairs with boxes and cases, and the drive outside filled up with a van and two cars. He knew it was the holidays because Poppy wasn't wearing her school clothes. He put his head rather anxiously in her lap.

'It's all right, Charley. We're going to the most lovely place. It's got palm trees and beautiful blue sea and sunshine. My father is going to work there, so I won't have to go to my boring school any more.' She bent down and kissed Freddie's nose and he kissed her back. But he still felt anxious.

She went on talking. 'We're going to fly in an aeroplane. I haven't been in one since I was a baby – before I knew you, Charley. Isn't that exciting? Dad said that you wouldn't be able to fly in the cabin with us, but they have people to look after dogs, so you will be fine.'

Although Freddie didn't understand what she was talking about, he knew that she was trying to reassure him and that meant that something was not quite right. Then they both heard Mrs Keeper calling Poppy. Poppy took his face between her two hands, pressing them against his whiskers, and then she kissed him a lot – starting with the top of his head and working down to his cold black nose, and then up and down each side of his face and he became aware that he was making small whimpering noises that didn't at all tell her what he felt, which was nothing but love. He knew then that Poppy was his life; to guard and care for, to follow and watch. Poppy was what he was for – if the world only had Poppy in it, it would be enough for him.

'Tell you what, Charley,' Poppy said, 'you have eyes that actually glow.'

It was the last thing she said to him. Mrs Keeper swept in, scolding as usual; she seized Poppy's arm and practically dragged her out of the room; she seemed to be in a particularly bad temper. Of course Charley started to follow them, but she slammed the door in his face. He scratched on the door and barked and barked, and then he heard Poppy crying and he scrabbled harder at the door, but it was no use. Some doors have handles that you can push down with your paw, but this door had a round handle that he couldn't manage. He heard noises in the hall, several voices besides Mrs Keeper's. He knew they were all going somewhere and taking Poppy with them. He ran to the other side of the room, where the window looked out on the place with the cars, and at that moment he heard the door handle to the room being turned and he dashed back, but the door didn't open and he heard Poppy burst into loud sobs and Mrs Keeper talking to her. Charley rushed back to the window. There was a ledge under it – too narrow for him to sit on, but if he put his front paws on it, he could see out. Mrs Keeper was now dragging Poppy to the car. Charley barked and barked and he knew Poppy heard him because she called his name, but Mrs Keeper stuffed her into the car and slammed the door and the man in the car drove off. Mrs Keeper stood watching the car till it disappeared out of sight. Then she turned back to the house: she had a horrible smile on her face and Charley knew she was wicked and he wanted to bite her. But Poppy had said that he would be going in the aeroplane with her and he trusted her. So he decided to be very meek and careful with Mrs Keeper as she seemed to be the only person who could take him to Poppy's aeroplane.

But she didn't, of course. She left him locked up in that room for hours, and although he felt too anxious to want any food he got terribly thirsty. He tried drinking out of a bowl with flowers in it, but it tasted horrible. In the end he lay down by the door so that if anyone opened it he could get out.

It was a very long time indeed before Mrs Keeper opened the door, but she seized Charley before he could escape her. She put the loop of a piece of rope around his neck that got too tight when she pulled it, which she did until he was nearly choking. Then she took his lovely collar off and threw it in the fireplace. Charley could not understand why she was doing these things, but he didn't have time to think, because she dragged him outside to her car, which was very small and filled with suitcases. She pushed him into the back and tied the rope to a door handle; it was very uncomfortable as she made the rope so short that he could not sit on the seat, nor could he lie on the floor properly because of all the luggage. *We must be going to the aeroplane*, he thought, because that was what Poppy had said would happen. Mrs Keeper drove for a long time; she was muttering to herself and Charley sensed that she was very angry about something. They drove through streets with houses everywhere and a great many cars and the air smelled dark brown and he began to feel sick.

He also began to know that she was not taking him to Poppy. He had always known that she did not like him, but now he felt her hatred: her mutterings sounded spiteful and he felt really frightened of her.

Eventually she stopped the car by a wall, got Charley out and dragged him through a door, the other side of which was a large building. Even before they entered, he was overwhelmed by the terrible smell – well, there were two smells really; one was a sort of cleaning odour – a bit like what they used to clean the lavatories in Poppy's house, only much, much stronger. The other was horrible in a quite different way – it was the awful smell like at the vet's, of animal anxiety and fear – only this was coming from many, many dogs. Charley made one desperate lunge to escape, but it only made the rope tighten around his neck till it nearly choked him again.

As they went through a second much larger door, Mrs Keeper bent down and loosened the rope. On the other side were a man and a woman. Mrs Keeper started talking to them in the smarmy way she did with Poppy's father, what Poppy had called her lying voice, and the woman wrote down some things, and then she gave Charley a pat on the head; he thought she was going to hit him and he cringed, and Mrs Keeper laughed in an artificial way and handed the rope to the man and then she went. It was a relief, but it was also awful, because she was Charley's last link with Poppy and how could these people who did not know either Poppy or him get him to her aeroplane?

Charley was panting from thirst and the woman

got a good large bowl of cold water for him, and he drank nearly all of it.

They both talked to him kindly while they removed the rope and put a collar on. Charley felt then that if only he could tell them what he wanted they would help him, but of course he couldn't.

They took him to a small room and lifted him onto a black table and a man in a white coat looked into his ears and mouth and put some cold thing on bits of his chest and then felt all along his body and he thought they all seemed pleased.

Then the woman led him down a passage and through a door at the end. The moment she opened the door a frenzy of barking broke out – it was deafening. Dogs shouting, 'Look at me! . . . Help me! . . . Let me out of here! . . . Please come to me! . . . I want to go home!' Some of them were just howling. They were all in small cages down both sides of the passage and they all rushed towards the woman and Charley with awful hope, standing on their hind legs with their faces pressed against the bars. All the cages seemed full, but at the end there was a bigger cage with just one large black dog lying in it. His coat was curly with bits of grey in it. He did not bark, but got to his feet and walked stiffly towards the woman who had opened the cage door. She stroked his head and talked to him while he gazed at her. He looked as though he understood everything she was saying.

Then she unclipped Charley's lead and pushed him gently into the cage, said something to both of them and left.

For a minute they both stood looking at each other and then did the usual sniff dogs do with strangers. Charley asked the black dog his name.

'Alphonse. I'm French – a poodle, in case you didn't know.'

'I thought you were. A poodle, I mean; I didn't know about the French part.'

'And you are a lurcher. Your name?'

'Charley. I'm not meant to be here, I—'

'Everyone says that,' Alphonse said wearily.

'No, but I'm meant to be in an aeroplane with Poppy. But a wicked woman didn't take me to the aeroplane – she brought me here. Poppy said we were going to a beautiful island and she's always truthful; it's horrible Mrs Keeper who looked after the house where Poppy lived who lied. She hated me.'

'Was she meant to be going with you?'

'No. It was just Poppy, her father and me.'

'Ah, well – doubtless she was jealous. Anyway, you won't be staying long here.'

'How do you know?'

'Lurchers never do. Also, the lady who brought you said it wouldn't be for long.'

While Charley was wondering how on earth he could know what she'd meant, Alphonse said, 'I can't speak it, of course, but over the years I have learned to understand a good deal of Masterspeak. I am highly intelligent, you see. And for the last eighteen and a half months I have had a good deal of time on my paws. I am going to lie down because my bones ache and I am unusually old. You'll find water in the corner over there if you want a drink. There's no more food till breakfast.'

Charley was very tired, and his stomach rumbled because he was hungry, but it was a great relief to have someone to talk to. The barking had died down – there were dogs whimpering and whining a bit: occasionally, an Alsatian a few cages along made a desolate howling sound. Every now and then he could hear an aeroplane, and each time he thought of Poppy flying miles away from him and expecting to find him there when the aeroplane landed, and how she would feel when she discovered that he wasn't, and this made a pain in his tummy and he was too sad to sleep.

'I can feel you are very miserable. You'd better tell me about it – get it off your chest.'

Alphonse spoke very quietly; after a questioning look, Charley moved until their noses were almost touching.

'We don't want to wake the others,' Alphonse said.

So Charley told him the whole story. Mainly he told him about Poppy and how much they loved one another. Poppy had no mother, he explained, and her father was so busy organising things that he had very little time left for her. This also meant that he had never seemed to notice how horrible Mrs Keeper really was, as she always smiled at him and called him Sir Edward. As Charley told it, he could see that she had been so angry because she wasn't asked to go to the island with them. Charley said that he knew she had always hated him, but how could she be so cruel to Poppy?

Alphonse simply looked at him pityingly. 'Human nature,' he said, 'tends to be worse than any other kind. I tremble to think what they would be like if they didn't have us.' He shifted his position on the hard floor. He was clearly in pain.

'There are exceptions, of course. You have Poppy, and I have Major Hawkins Jones M.C.'

Charley tried hard to understand this. He didn't have Poppy – she was miles away – and there was no sign of Major Hawk— or whatever his name was. But before he could ask, Alphonse said, 'Major Hawkins Jones is dead. We were taking our usual walk on Hampstead Heath, when he seemed to stagger and then he dropped down. He was trying to breathe. Then he just said, "Sorry, old bloke – afraid this is it." He tried to reach out to touch me, but his arm just flopped, and his head fell to one side and he didn't move any more.'

Charley was so shocked that he couldn't speak. He noticed that Alphonse was trembling and his large brown eyes were full of grief. 'What did you do?' he asked at last.

'I stayed with him, of course. It was winter, and there was a frost. To begin with I thought I could revive him if I lay across his chest to warm him up, but he got colder and colder. In the end I just lay beside him with my head against his face. It got dark and started to snow. I tried licking the snow off his face, but in the end I got too cold to move.' He was silent for a while as they both thought of that dreadful night.

Eventually Charley, unable to bear it, asked, 'Then what happened?'

'People came. A keeper saw us and then several people came with a large white van and lifted my Major onto a bed thing. I tried to stop them, but I was frozen stiff and I couldn't stand – only growl. I wanted to go with them, but my legs wouldn't work properly. I whined and begged them to take me too, but of course, although I understand Masterspeak, I can't speak it. They put me in another car and brought me here, to the refuge. I heard them saying that they hoped to find me a new home, but people don't want a really old dog (I'm fifteen) so I've just stayed. They gave me this larger cage in the end because I'm good at calming down any very nervous new arrivals. Like you. That woman who brought you in sometimes takes me out for walks, but I'm so stiff and sore in my legs that I don't really enjoy it. And I don't mind being shut up. I don't really care about anything without Major Hawkins Jones. A dog doesn't have much to live for when his person is dead.'

Charley felt very sad for poor Alphonse, but he was also confused. 'You said I had Poppy and you had Major Hawk—' he couldn't manage the whole name – 'Jones. But you haven't got him if he is dead!'

'Oh yes, I will always have him. He is always in my mind, you see. I think of him all the time. But of course it isn't the same with you. Your Poppy is alive, and you have a chance – a small chance, I admit – that she will find you. But even if she doesn't, you will always know that you love her.'

Charley wanted to ask how Poppy could possibly find him, but Alphonse looked so weary and sad that he simply put his head on the poodle's outstretched paws in silent sympathy, and they both slept.

Charley was woken early the next morning by the other dogs shouting with excitement because a man was wheeling in a trolley that smelled strongly of food. Food! He realised that he was famished, as he had not eaten anything since the half-biscuit that Poppy had given him at breakfast yesterday. (It seemed far longer than that – more like weeks.)

It took him a few seconds to realise where he was – in this place with the awful smells of dog fear, dog excitement, dog desperation. Everyone seemed to be barking, yapping, yelping – some from excitement at the smell of food, some because they wanted someone to talk to them, some because they simply wanted to be let out – to be free. Charley felt something of all these things, but at that moment food was the most urgent.

Alphonse and he were at the end of the aisle and were the last to be fed. The man put two bowls in their cage and filled up their water bowl from a jug. The barking was followed by the fainter sounds of the inmates' metal tags clinking against their bowls. Neither Charley nor his new friend had barked, and the man gave each of them a pat on the head. The food was mostly very dull biscuits with some chunks of tinned meat. It did not taste like the food he had been used to, but he was too hungry to care. When he had finished, he noticed that Alphonse had only picked a few pieces out of his bowl and was drinking quite a lot of water. Then the poodle wandered to a far corner at the back of the cage and squatted. 'This is where we do this sort of thing,' he said. 'Don't want the place to become a pigsty.'

Charley didn't know what a pigsty was, but he didn't want their cage to become anything that Alphonse didn't like. So he took the hint.

Then the moment that nothing was actually happening, his misery rolled over him like a horrible fog. He had lost Poppy and he could not think how to find her. If she had stayed in the country, he thought, he would have found her somehow. He would not have stopped searching until there was nowhere left for her to be except the place where in the end he would find her.

He thought about this meeting – how she would be – asleep in a wood, on her pony looking for him, in the potting shed where they used to hide from Mrs Keeper when it was raining . . .

'It's all right, old bloke.' And he realised that the soft howling noise was him and there was a horrible ache in his chest.

Alphonse had moved up to him and was sympathising with his kind eyes. 'It will get better,' he said. 'They'll find you a good home.'

Charley wanted to say that the only good home for him would be with Poppy, but he was too choked up to speak.

'I tell you what we'll do. We'll play a little game together . . .'

So they did. For the next few days they took it in turns to tell each other exactly what their days had been like with their beloved owners. Charley found it comforting to be able to tell Alphonse every little thing about Poppy that came into his mind (and he was surprised how much that was), and he learned a very great deal about life with Major Hawkins Jones.

'Every morning,' Alphonse would begin in a

dreamy voice, 'the Major would let me out in the back garden of our flat, and when I came back there would be the wonderful smell of bacon frying. He always had a cooked breakfast – sometimes with tomatoes, sometimes with fried bread, but always bacon – except Sundays; he always had sausages on Sundays, and I got one as well. "There you are, old bloke," he would say when he'd cut it up for me.'

Charley interrupted to ask what old blokes were.

'Oh, they were the good people, the ones the Major approved of. There weren't many of them – the Major said a lot of them had died. Old blokes were good; then there were whipper-snappers, who were mostly young and made a noise, and then there were scum, and they were just plain awful. The Major used to read about them in his newspaper every morning while he was drinking his bright brown tea – I had a saucer of that as he thought it was good for my coat, but really I just liked having the same as him. We lived on our own except occasionally an old bloke would drop in for tea or another dark brown drink. But we really didn't need other people. Major Hawkins Jones got a large floppy paper every morning which he read, and then he did the crossword with a pencil on the paper. Judging from the bits he read aloud from the paper, no wonder it was called the *cross*word. Once he said that the whole country was going to the dogs; I could tell he felt this would be awful, and judging by most of the dogs I met on the Heath, I certainly wouldn't want everything going to them, but it worried me that he might think I was just one of them, which I wasn't. I was a poodle in a thousand.'

'But I suppose you couldn't tell him that.' By now Charley felt that Alphonse was the best dog he had ever met.

'I made myself clear. I looked at him for a long time without saying a word, and then I walked across the room and sat with my back to him until he came and apologised. "A figure of speech" he called it, but it didn't ring true to me: there are speeches with words and there are figures for things like how much money – am I boring you?'

'Only a bit.' Charley always tried to be honest, even if it was difficult – like now.

At that moment frenzied barking broke out because people were coming through the door at the far end of the passage.

'They're coming to look for a dog – to choose one and take it home with them, and all the dogs hope it will be them.'

'Might they choose you?' Charley felt suddenly frightened.

'No – they never choose me. I'm too old; not worth the vet's fees, I heard one of them say. They might choose you though.'

This was almost as alarming a prospect. 'I only want Poppy as my owner. She is my owner.'

'The trouble is,' Alphonse said sadly, 'that they have a choice, and we don't.'

Charley went to the back of the cage and pretended to be asleep. 'Lie in front of me,' he said. 'Then perhaps they won't notice me.'

At the end of the day three or four dogs had been chosen – people seemed to want small ones – but they did not leave their cages. 'They go and inspect the future owners' homes first. They take a lot of trouble.'

In the early evening the woman – Alphonse said she was called Anne – put them both on leads and took them for a walk in a small park nearby. Alphonse ambled – walks hurt his legs, he said, but Charley desperately wanted to stretch his, and pulled hard at his lead while trying to make reliable noises about coming back when he was called. 'Oh – all right then,' Anne said, and let him go. He did two galloping circuits around Anne and his friend, and then went back to them, hot and smug. 'What a good dog!' she said as she took them back.

Two more days went by like this. Charley learned a lot more about Major Hawkins Jones. He had a rather growly voice; he loved richly buttered crumpets, which they had for tea in winter, and very hot curries (Charley couldn't think what they were); he took ages to do the shopping while Alphonse sat outside the shops – 'Bit short of cash this week,' he would say almost every week. On Fridays they queued at the place where he got his pension money. That day he would usually buy a chop or a kipper, though mostly he ate beans or sardines on toast. But he always bought meat in tins for Alphonse, and biscuits and occasionally a bone if the butcher was in a good mood. Once a week he took his sheets and shirts and things to the launderette and they waited while things got washed and dried. They went for two walks on the Heath every day, and once a year they went to stay with the Major's sister Constance in a cottage in a place called Rye. Alphonse loved it there – the different walks and getting to swim in the sea and at least three bones in the week that they were there. But the Major had what he called pros and cons: he went through them every year while he stuffed things into his very heavy leather suitcase that had to be strapped shut with one of his belts as the clasps to shut it were broken. The pros were lots of hot cooked food: shepherd's pie, kedgeree, toad-in-the-hole, rice pudding, blackberry-and-apple crumble – things like that. A very nice pub down the lane where he could have a pint with a lot of other sensible blokes who thought the world was not what it used to be; his sister to whom he could read bits out of the paper that enraged him. Cons: Constance went in for some newfangled contraption – duvets, they were called, instead of sensible blankets and an eiderdown. Every year she presented him with either three pairs of socks or a pullover she had knitted for him; the socks were of very scratchy wool that brought him out in a rash, and the pullovers were several sizes too small, or else, when he protested, so enormous that they hung around him like a tent. He had to be grateful for these offerings. But the worst con was the awful cat. They both hated the cat, a huge ginger with a bright pink nose and a shady expression. In spite of the endless saucers of food that he demolished several times a day, he tried to steal Alphonse's daily meal (he only had one) and at night he brought in endless unfortunate mice, young birds and once even a grass snake in a helpless swag between his jaws. He was a bully and a killer.

They also discussed Charley's situation at length and Alphonse, after some thought, said, 'You know, she might call people here and ask whether you've turned up.'

'How will I ever know that?'

'Well, they'll ask what your name is and then they'll come and call you Charley, and then they will know. It's just a thought,' he added, as he saw – and could hardly bear – the expression of wild hope in Charley's eyes. 'Don't count on it – it's only a small idea,' he said later.

Charley said that he wouldn't, but of course he did.

On the third day more people came looking for dogs, among them two oldish-looking women.

One of them, seeing Charley curled up at the back of the cage as usual exclaimed, 'Oh – a lurcher! I've always wanted a lurcher. They are so heraldic – like medieval embroidery!' She asked Anne if she could have a better look, and Anne came and made him come out of the cage, holding him by his collar. Charley stood trembling with his tail between his legs. 'Poor thing! He looks so miserable. He clearly needs a good home!' The woman stroked Charley, ruffling up his fur the wrong way; he didn't like the smell of her at all. The woman talked to Anne for a bit and then they went away.

'That was a near thing,' Charley said.

But Alphonse said he didn't think so at all. 'They've agreed to go and look at her home, and if they think it's all right, she'll take you. She said she lived in a large house near a park and it has a back garden. It could be worse, you know.'

'No, it couldn't. I don't like her and I'd far rather be with you anyway. If she'd take both of us—'

'My dear old bloke, she won't do that. I told you

– I really don't care. I'll miss you, of course, but don't worry about me.'

Charley was full of horribly mixed feelings. He knew it was good to be called a bloke, but he realised that when he had said that he would far rather be with Alphonse, he was thinking only of himself and hardly at all about his lonely intelligent heartsick old friend. He wanted to howl – about everything: about Poppy being gone, about his first real friendship being stopped, about how awful it must be for Alphonse with Major Hawkins Jones being dead . . .

'Would you like a bit of a groom?'

He knew that Alphonse – like most dogs – had bits around the bottom of his ears that his paws and tongue couldn't reach.

'Don't mind if I do.'

Charley recognised that this must be one of the Major's sayings; he often couldn't understand what on earth they actually meant, but in this case he could tell that Alphonse would like a bit of grooming, so he set about it.

* * *

Two more days went peacefully by; more people came and looked at more dogs, and one rather dangerous-looking man said he would like Charley, but when he had gone Alphonse said that Anne had said he was already bespoke.

'It means that you are going to that woman,' Alphonse told him, and indeed, that is what happened. The next morning he just had time to touch his friend's nose before he was reluctantly dragged away. 'You'll be all right, old bloke,' were the poodle's last words, as Charley was led down the long passage back to the place where Mrs Keeper had left him.

When Charley was unhappy and afraid, he shook. He stood now – trembling. He looked at Anne, silently beseeching her to save him, but she, all smiles like his new owner, was busy fixing the brand-new collar that the owner had brought. Her name seemed to be Hoot, or Coot, as Anne kept repeating that when they talked –

and did not seem to notice how he was feeling. Hoot or Coot kept patting him and pushing his fur the wrong way, and when she tried to lead him out of the door he wouldn't budge, and Anne had to take over. Do you know what it's like when you feel rotten and sad about something but somehow you can't tell anyone about it? Well, Charley was like that. He was leaving the last place that had any connection at all with Poppy – Mrs Keeper, horrid though she was, had brought him from Poppy's house to here – and he was leaving the first dog friend he had ever had – Alphonse. He felt his heart would break.

Anne put him in the back seat of Hoot's car and gave him a final pat. He licked her hand – giving her one last desperate look – but she shut the car door and stood waving at Hoot as the car started its journey.

The car smelled strongly of Hoot – a mixture of her hot skin smell and a kind of sweetish scent, plus wafts of tobacco that reminded him of Poppy's father, and that made him feel sad even more than he felt sick. He sat bolt upright during the drive with his nose resting on the crack of the open window. Something told him that he'd better watch where they were going, in case he got a chance to escape.

Eventually the car stopped outside a tall house with railings and steps up to the door.

'Come along, Muffin!' Hoot cried as she dragged him out.

'Your name is Muffin,' she told him, and kept repeating the idiotic name. Alphonse had said that it was a large house with a garden. What no one had mentioned was that Hoot or Coot lived in a very small flat on the ground floor of the large house. There were two rooms – one that looked out onto the street and one at the back that looked out onto the garden. There was a small kitchen and a tiny bathroom. The whole place was rather dark and smelled – apart from Hoot's smells – of damp earth.

He stood, shivering, while she unclipped his lead and fetched two bowls from the kitchen, one with water and the other with some food. 'There you are, Muffin.' She took him by the collar and dragged him over to the bowls, trying to push his nose into the food, but he didn't feel like eating. He sensed that this was making her cross, but then her telephone rang and she talked into it for a long time. He looked around the small back room that contained a bed and other furniture and, in the corner near the window that looked onto the garden, a large cardboard box with a blanket in it. After a bit, he lay in that.

She seemed pleased about that, and came over and ruffled his fur; 'Good boy, Muffin.'

Later she opened the window (which came down to the ground) and let him out into the garden. It had walls down its long sides and some kind of fencing at the bottom. He looked carefully to see if there was any way out, but there wasn't, unless he could jump over the fence, but there was a steep sloping bed in front of it that meant he would have to jump from a standing position. Also the fence was covered with some climbing plant that, when he nosed it, turned out to be thorny.

'Muffin! Muffin?'

She was calling him. He had a quick pee and, after leaving it long enough for her to realise that Muffin was not his name, he walked slowly back to the house. 'Good boy!' she said in her treacly voice.

She talks to me as though I am a stupid baby, he whined miserably. *Poppy never talked to me like that. Nor Alphonse.* At the thought of them, a fresh wave of misery overcame him. As soon as he was inside, she shut the window and left the flat. He had a drink of water, but couldn't face his food. He heard her car drive off and then all was silent. He went miserably to his box and, sitting upright in it, he lifted his head and howled.

It was hours before she came back, and he pretended to be asleep. As she undressed she kept saying he was a good boy and she came and ruffled his fur up the wrong way before getting into her bed. He didn't sleep much, but when he did doze off, dreams of escaping flitted through his mind, and he woke because he was twitching with the excitement of bounding along – free. It wasn't much fun waking up in the cardboard box with the Hoot smell, which seemed worse in the morning.

Hoot let him out in the garden, and when he came back she was dressed and drinking some black drink that he recognised as coffee. She put some food down for him and then left. He heard her car starting up and driving away. He was alone in this silent locked-up place.

Hours later she came back, put him on a lead and walked him in the street for a bit and then he was back in the flat again and she went off in her car again. She didn't come back for hours. In the evening she returned and took him for another dreary walk. He couldn't even run, which would have cheered him up a bit, because she never let him off the lead.

And that was what the days were like. He ate hardly any food and simply couldn't respond to her advances – patting him and telling him what a good Muffin he was. He sensed that this was making her cross, but he really didn't care.

And then, out of the blue, he had an enormous stroke of luck. Or possible luck. Two men – an old one and a young one – turned up one morning before Hoot left. Hoot seemed to know them well. She took them to the kitchen. He heard her talking about him and then talking a lot more, and then she rushed out, rushed back and threw them some keys. 'Goodbye, Muffin,' she called as she left the flat.

He had been lying quietly in his box, but as soon as she had gone, he went to the kitchen. He wanted the men to like him, so he wagged his tail and looked into their faces. They stroked him and spoke in kindly voices. The younger one, who was rather spotty, was making tea, and the older one, who had a beard, was unpacking a bag full of hammers and things. Then Beard said something to Spotty. Spotty got up from the floor where he had been laying out parts of a washing machine and went out of the flat. Charley followed him to the door, which he left open, and watched to see if he left the main front door open as well. He did, but only a crack, and Charley was afraid that by the time he would have managed to push it wide enough to get through Spotty would be coming back up the path that led to the street. So he sat by the flat door, trying to look as though the last thing he wanted to do was escape.

He was quite right to wait. Spotty came back very quickly; he carried a paper bag that smelled delicious. He went to the kitchen and Charley followed him to the door. Beard was sitting on the floor cleaning something with a small stiff brush. A mug of steaming dark brown tea sat on the floor between his legs. After Spotty had poured himself another steaming mug, he sat opposite him and unwrapped the contents of the paper bag. The smell became unbearably wonderful, and Charley realised how hungry he was. He edged himself into the kitchen – there was only just room for him – and gazed longingly at the stack of thick meat sandwiches that Spotty and Beard were chewing. He made a tiny whimpering sound. It worked. Spotty broke off pieces from his sandwich and gave them to him. Charley's tail beat the floor in gratitude. By the time they had finished, he had had the best part of two sandwiches. He licked both their hands to thank them, and they patted him and said he was a good dog. He went into the front room and had a long drink of water, and then lay down by the door with his head between his paws. He was much too nervous and excited to sleep as he realised that his one chance of escape would be when the men had finished their work and went back out to their van.

He was wrong. He heard them clattering about with their tools, and then they sounded as though they were arguing, and finally as though they were having a full-scale row. Then Spotty came out – you couldn't see his spots because he was so red in the face from rage. He stormed out of the flat, leaving both doors wide open. Charley didn't hesitate. He slipped through the flat door, and the front one. Then he paused. The back doors of the van were open, but all he could see of Spotty was his bottom and his boots. He was burrowing well into the back of the van.

Charley ran – as fast as he had ever run in his life. He did not stop until he was several streets away from Hoot's prison flat. His instinct had been to go back to Poppy's home, but he told himself that a) she would not be there, and b) horrible Mrs Keeper might be.

Eventually he reached the small park where Hoot had taken him once for a dreary walk on the lead. He found some bushes to hide in while he got his breath back and thought what to do.

This did not take him long. He knew – almost at once – that he must get back to the refuge place to be with Alphonse, his only friend, who at least knew how badly he was missing Poppy. It seemed a long way away, but he was sure that somehow he would find it.

He waited until dusk before he set out. He no longer trusted any people, and he was especially afraid of people in cars in case they were Hoot coming to look for him. Mostly he trotted purposefully in what he thought was the right direction, but whenever he saw anyone he ran down the nearest side street. When it got dark and the street lights came on, there was nothing for it but to run. After some crashing noises in the sky it began to rain. The rain got worse and he was soon soaked, but the good thing about this was that there were hardly any people in the streets, and they were all too concerned with getting out of the wet to notice him. He ran for miles until he was really tired and thirsty. He drank some water out of quite a nice puddle, but the moment he stopped running he began to shiver. Then, suddenly his nose picked up the smells of the refuge place, and there was the wall with the gate in it that Hoot had taken him through. He knew he could not jump over the wall, as apart from being too high, it had an extra fence of wire on top of the brick. He was shaking with cold now, but the rain had stopped and it began to be less dark. How could he get in? Then he remembered that Mrs Keeper had pressed a knob and talked to the gate and it had said something back and then opened. He stood on his hind legs to find the knob – yes! There it was – a round thing with a button in the middle. He tried pushing it with his nose, but that didn't work. He tried leaping up to push the knob, but his paws were the wrong shape to get at the button. He could not think what to do. It was getting light quite quickly now; the street lamps had gone out and there began to be traffic – cars and buses and people on bicycles. He was terribly afraid that Hoot would turn up and stuff him into her horrid-smelling car. He was shaking with cold, his coat had not dried and he felt too weak to go on trying to press the difficult button. His despair was so great that when he saw two oldish women walking along the pavement towards him he decided on a final desperate plan. When they were a few yards away, he began scrabbling at the door and making noises that were a mixture of whining and yelps. They stopped. They made kindly noises, and one of them patted him. Then, wonderfully, one of them pushed the button, and, after a pause, he heard Anne's voice. Then the door opened, and he bounded in – up the path to the second door, which he pushed open. This final effort was too much for him, and he collapsed.

When he came to, he was on the table with the man in a white coat talking to Anne. He heard them mention Alphonse, whereupon he got to his feet, wagging his tail and looking into Anne's face. 'If only you'd understand, I'm begging you to take me to him! Begging you!'

She did understand. The man lifted him off the table, Anne clipped a lead onto his collar and led (or rather he led her) to the door on the other side of which were the dogs' cages. Wafts of

Alphonse's scent came to him and he strained at his lead. The noise that all the other dogs were making meant nothing; he was whimpering from excitement and the joy of being with his friend again.

Alphonse was lying in a huddled heap at the very back of his cage. He seemed to be asleep, and even when Charley called him, he still lay there with his eyes shut. Anne undid his lead and let him into the cage. As he reached Alphonse – saying, 'It's me – Charley' – the poodle opened his eyes, and his face, which had looked as sad and dejected as his whole body, changed to a kind of dazed delight.

'I thought I was dreaming you. Didn't want to wake up, old bloke.' The fur around his eyes, Charley noticed, was wet.

Anne, who had been watching them, pulled a small rough towel out of her overall pocket and gave Charley a quick rub-down which made him feel much warmer. 'Breakfast soon,' she said; 'and you jolly well eat it, Alphonse.'

'Lie against me, old bloke, and you'll soon get warm.' He put a large protective paw around his friend. Charley noticed that he could feel Alphonse's ribs. 'Been off my food lately,' said Alphonse.

'So have I.'

'She brought you back then?'

'No, I escaped. It was all horrible so I came back here: to be with you.'

Alphonse gave a deep sigh of content. 'A couple of bony old blokes, aren't we?'

Charley didn't reply. He buried his nose deep into the thick curly hair of his friend's shoulder and fell instantly asleep. He was woken by the clamour of breakfast. Everybody was shouting – about food, and how they wanted to get out, they weren't meant to be here – all the usual stuff. When the trolley got to them, the boy who usually did breakfast came into their cage with two bowls, which he put in the usual place, and as he went back to get the jug of water he said something to

Alphonse. Charley, who was already attacking his bowl, looked to see if the poodle was following suit, but he wasn't.

'Don't you want your breakfast?'

'Not much. Not really.'

'Yes, you do. Got to keep your strength up. The Major wouldn't like you not eating.'

This made Alphonse get painfully to his feet. His back legs were trembling and his coat looked poor.

'You're quite right. "None of that nonsense," he used to say. He didn't approve of nonsense, and it seemed to be all over the place. Once we were in a shop getting me a new collar and they offered a lovely red one, which, as I am French, I thought would be just right with my black fur, but he said that was nonsense too, and he bought me a brown one, same as usual.' Talking about the Major seemed to animate him, and he walked shakily to his bowl and started eating. Charley, who had finished his quickly, sat beside Alphonse telling him rather sternly to eat everything up. Then they both had a good drink.

'Well – now we'd better review the situation.'

'What situation?' Charley felt full of food and warm and nearly happy, and not very keen on a situation because they always seemed to be worrying.

'Well, this Hook or Crook person will come looking for you, won't she?'

He hadn't thought of that. 'She'll never think I would get here. It's miles away. She's not a dog.'

'She might easily think that someone found you wandering and bunged you in here.'

This gave him a moment of sheer panic. 'If she comes near me, I'll bite her. I'll growl to give warning, and then I'll BITE her!'

'No, you won't. You'll cringe. You'll lie down with your tail between your legs and you'll whine.'

'Why will I? I'm quite brave enough to bite her.'

'My dear old bloke, you'll cringe and whine

because then Anne will see that you are afraid of her, and you're afraid of her because she has been treating you badly. They never let people take dogs who do that. It's your best hope.'

Charley was overcome with affection and respect. 'I would never have thought of that. You really are a poodle in a thousand. TEN thousand!'

'I know I am. The Major recognised that. It was merely my sense of style that he didn't altogether grasp. Not a drop of – he called it frog – blood in his veins.'

Charley didn't understand that at all. Why would a poodle have any frog's blood? Anyway . . . 'I'll cringe,' he said.

'Show me!'

'That's not a really cringing cringe,' he said, after Charley had done his best.

'Well – you show me!'

Instantly Alphonse cowered away from him, his whole body abject with fear, his usually kind brown eyes rolling and showing the whites as though in panic, and uttering small whimpering cries of terror: 'Please don't hit me again; I beg you, beseech you – don't!

'More like that,' he said in his ordinary voice.

Charley was deeply impressed. 'What does beseech mean?'

'It means kind of double beg. Now, you have another go.'

So then they played a game of taking it in turns to frighten each other until Charley got quite good at it and Alphonse said that he was tired and needed his rest. 'At least we're prepared,' he said.

'For the worst?'

'It's the only thing we can prepare for. It comes from being a dog. No power. And precious little choice.'

'We can hope for the best.' Charley was sleepy now and did not at all want to think about the worst.

* * *

Anne took them for a brief walk. Alphonse tried to run so that Charley could get some exercise, but Charley stuck to walking or a sedate trot to suit Alphonse. They both enjoyed the fresher air, and Alphonse said that while Anne had stroked Charley's head, she'd said he would never have to go back to 'that woman' again. When she stroked Alphonse's head she said, 'You two; you're inseparable, aren't you?' They both kissed her hands and wagged their tails and Charley stood on his hind legs because he wanted to put his arms around her neck, but she just smiled and wouldn't let him. When they got back their cage had been cleaned out and there was nice cold water in their bowl. There was the usual shouting and yelping from the cages – 'What about me? Let me out! I want to go home!' – but Charley had become used to it, and anyway it died down as soon as Anne had collected the next group of dogs for their walk.

They had a short sleep comfortably curled up

together, and when they woke Alphonse proposed a game.

'It's called the best and the worst,' he said. 'You think of the best that could happen, and then I think of the worst.'

Charley thought as hard as he could.

'Poppy coming back and finding us and taking both of us in the aeroplane to her island.'

'Mrs Keeper and Hoot creeping back here in the night and dognapping us.'

Charley felt the fur on the back of his neck stand on end.

'My turn now. Major Hawkin Jones's sister suddenly turning up and saying she wants two dogs to protect her from wicked people and we are just the ticket.'

'The sister turns up but says she can't afford to keep two dogs, so she takes you and I'm left here.'

'The trouble is,' Charley said, after the true misery of being in the refuge without Alphonse had struck him, 'that the Worst seems so much more likely than the Best.'

'That's a dog's life. Do you think you could deal with the fur at the back of my ears? And I'll try to think of a game that's more cheerful.'

So Charley set about grooming his friend (whose fur had got into a sad state in his absence), finishing by washing his face with such affectionate vigour that Alphonse ended up on his back with his paws boxing Charley's face. After a bit of rolling about, Alphonse said he gave in and they both had another good sleep.

Charley dreamed. He was in his bed in Poppy's room and she was calling him; 'Charley! Up, Charley; you know you can do it!'

He woke quite suddenly, and just had time to realise that he was in the cage with Alphonse – that he had been dreaming – when he saw that Anne had come into the cage.

'Charley . . . ?' she was saying. 'Are you by any chance Charley?'

He was – indeed he was. He rushed to her – he was saying, *yes! yes! yes!* a hundred times – wagging his tail, licking her hands, his eyes glowing with excitement and joy. He was Charley – Poppy must have found him – he would soon be with Poppy again . . . He turned to his friend; Alphonse was sitting bolt upright gazing at him, an expression in his large brown eyes that Charley had never seen before – of so much love and sadness . . . He went up to his friend and touched his nose.

'It's the best,' Alphonse said, his voice so husky and small that Charley could hardly hear him.

Then they both became aware of the man in a white coat standing outside the cage. He and Anne started talking, and Alphonse, his ears pricked, listened. What he afterwards told Charley was something like this.

'You see what I mean? They really should stay together.'

'My dear Anne, they won't want to take on a totally unknown dog – an old dog at that.'

'We could at least ask them. Explain.'

'We could. If only they had someone in this country to see the poodle, they just might agree – but as it is . . .'

'Well, they said they'd call us to see whether we'd identified the lurcher; I could talk to them then. The little girl will be so pleased I think she would agree to anything.'

'She may, but unfortunately little girls don't make that sort of decision. You'll just have to find the poodle another friend . . .' They were walking away and Alphonse couldn't hear any more.

The two dogs looked at each other. Then Charley, who had not lost his exhilaration, said, 'They were talking about you coming with me! Weren't they?'

'Talking about it, yes. But the man is quite right: Poppy's father won't see the point of having a second dog – and he's the one who'll decide.'

'If only I could talk to Poppy – get her to see how much it matters . . .'

'But you can't. You can't talk to her any more than I can. We're not in charge, Charley. We're dogs. We can't choose things. It's all part of being a dog.'

A shock. He had always known that he loved

Poppy, but now he knew that he also loved his friend. It was like having a second heart, and the vision of being led away from him, leaving him lonely and sad, was more than he could bear. He made a heroic decision.

'I won't go without you,' he said.

The poodle, who had been lying with his head between his paws, lifted it now to look at him.

'My dear old bloke, I've been trying to explain: it's no good you saying things like that. You can't choose what happens and nor can I.' He put out a shaky paw to stroke Charley's face. 'But I shall always remember that you said that. Always. It was brave and charming of you.' A moment later he said, 'I'm tired, Charley, really bone tired.'

They had a sleep, as they always did, with Charley's arm around Alphonse's shoulder and his head burrowed into the soft curly fur of his chest . . .

* * *

He was running on dazzling white sand, and Alphonse was running as well – splashing easily and fast through the shallow edge of a greeny blue sea, and a yellow silver sun was pouring down onto their hot fur, and he was completely happy because he knew that Alphonse felt the same.

Then, just as he began to realise that the hot sunlight was fading, the sea and the sky becoming darker, Alphonse left his side and plunged into the sea. Charley barked, but there was no answer, and almost at once he could not even see the dark head of his friend. He ran into the sea to follow him, but at that moment it became completely dark, everything black, and he was conscious of feeling bitterly cold, and when he shouted despairingly for Alphonse, his voice was so small that he could scarcely hear it. Gradually a grey light was there, he was shivering, and everything around him seemed enormous . . .

* * *

'That seems to have been quite a serious adventure.'

He licked one of his soaking paws; it tasted of salt. Two black eyes were regarding him; it was the sorcerer toad. He was speechless with shock. He wasn't Charley any more, and just when everything had seemed so marvellous, he had lost his friend Alphonse – and he was back to being a mouse. Tears rushed to his eyes; he longed with all his heart to be Charley and to be with his friend.

'Your time was up. You didn't remember about Freddie at all, did you? Well, I didn't want you to. This time I wanted you to really understand about being a dog.'

'I want to go back to that. I want to be back with Alphonse.'

The toad waited while he wept. Then he said, quite gently for a toad, 'I'm afraid it isn't possible to be Charley forever.'

'Why? Is he dead? Are they both dead?'

'No, no. They are on their way to the island, to Poppy.'

'So Alphonse won't feel that I've left him?'

'No. He's still with Charley. You were just Charley for a week, which is what you asked for. And thanks – partly to you – they – all three of them – will be together. Isn't that good?'

He thought of Alphonse and how much he loved Charley.

He thought of Charley and how much he loved Poppy.

Then he thought that if you loved someone, you wanted them to be happy, and if they were all together on the island, they would be. He blinked the last tears from his eyes.

'Yes,' he said; 'it is good. 'It's what I wanted most, for us – I mean them – to be together. It's just – well – I don't know. I'm not looking forward to being the same old feeble mouse.'

The toad's mouth widened into what Freddie had come to recognise was a smile.

'Ah! But you won't be.'

'I don't want to be turned into another some-one else!'

'I thought I'd made it clear that I'm not spending any more of my sorcery on that. You won't be the mouse you were before. You will be a very different mouse now. Think of all you've learned.'

Freddie tried to think, but he couldn't come up with anything. Then he said, 'Well, when I was a tiger I was always hungry and there was nobody to talk to: not at all like when I was Charley.'

'But when you were a dog, you had no choice about what happened to you. Your friend Alphonse – a most intelligent dog – pointed that out to you several times.'

'I know. He was a poodle in a thousand. Ten thousand. I shall always miss him. And Poppy. I loved them both, you see.' And his eyes, already sore with crying, filled again with scalding tears.

'There, you see? You didn't know anything about love until you became Charley. Stop crying, Freddie, or you won't listen to me properly.'

Freddie took a deep breath and managed to stop, but this gave him hiccoughs.

The toad waited a bit for them to stop, but they didn't.

'If you don't stop that silly noise, Freddie, I shall give you an eNORmouse fright.'

Freddie, who was frightened at the thought of an eNORmouse fright, stopped at once.

'I want you to consider the advantages of being a mouse.'

There was a pause while Freddie battled with not hiccoughing.

'You said that as a tiger you were lonely. A mouse need never be lonely. As a dog you had no choice about what happened to you. As a mouse you have any amount of choice. Naturally, if you don't recognise these advantages you are going to feel discontented and sorry for yourself. You have proved that you are quite brave – even enterprising – think of your escape from Hoot – but the moment you get home, you mooch around complaining about everything. True?'

Freddie nodded miserably. *Brave . . . enterprising* – he clung on to those more cheering remarks about his character.

'I suppose I must just make the best of it,' he said, wondering how on earth he could do that.

'I'm coming to that. That house you live in—'

'It's not a house, it's a very small flat. It's No. 16, Skirting Board West at No. 3, The Grove.'

'And No. 3, The Grove is a very large house. But you've never explored it, have you? You've never been further than the ground floor.'

'No, I haven't. My mother always said it was far too dangerous.'

'That is a mere mother's remark. All very well for an ordinary mouse. But you are no longer ordinary, Freddie; you have had adventures. You won't find another mouse within miles who has been a tiger and a dog. So now you must do the next thing.'

'The next thing?' It made him tremble to think of what that might be.

'Explore the house: every floor of it. See what

you can find. It's time you had a home of your own.'

There was a silence while a sleepy fly got too near and the toad's tongue shot out and devoured it.

'I have often wondered why the general intelligence of flies doesn't improve, since my kind take such a heavy toll of the fools.' He sighed – a rather squelching sound – and Freddie took a step backwards. 'However, it is fortunate for me that they continue to abound. Now – back to you. What about this new adventure? I know you think you are brave, so how about proving it? I've taken a great deal of trouble over you, and I certainly don't want all my sorcery wasted. To put it quite simply, are you a tiger or a dog or a MOUSE?'

And Freddie, without hesitation, said, 'I'm a MOUSE.' And to his amazement he felt quite proud to say it.

'Splendid. Off you go. You can report back to me if you like. Retirement has its disadvantages

– I shall be rather short of news. Not bad news, mind – the other kind.'

'Thank you very much for all your help.'

'Ah! Gratitude. Another thing you have learned. Your character is much improved. Now go off and learn to be enterprising.'

Chapter Six

On his way home, Freddie decided that he'd better do something enterprising before facing his mother. Being enterprising meant being brave, and he decided that it would be easier to be brave if he wasn't quite so hungry. The rubbish bins would probably be the easiest place for that.

It was early evening, and the door separating the back garden from the front, where the bins were, was ajar. The bins had been recently emptied, but as usual they had been overflowing, and he quickly found the remains of a chicken carcass and dragged it under the bushes. It was a good thing he did: people kept coming through the gate from the street to go up the front steps of No. 3. They were coming back from what they did all day, and would now be cooking, so the kitchen was out of bounds to mice until much later. But he was no longer mice; he was a MOUSE. He looked up at the enormous house; his heart was pounding. Lights had come on on all the floors except the very top one, that had only one window under a small pointed roof. It was now or never.

He got onto the ground floor – the one with the kitchen well known to him. He got to that quite easily because the back door had a gap under it. There were people crashing about in the kitchen, but the flight of stairs up to the next floor was empty. He stopped on the landing of the next floor because the blast of noise almost knocked him out. Someone shouted angrily from below and then doors were slammed, and the music – for that was what his mother had said it was called – got quieter. He waited a bit: the next flight of stairs confronted him. *I'll explore the rooms in the daytime when the people are all out.* The thought that they might not all be out occurred to him, but he decided that it was not a brave thought so he stopped thinking it.

The second flight was steeper than the first, and he arrived on the second landing breathless. The people on this floor had their sitting-room door open: they were sitting on chairs watching a box that had a man talking. They all had their backs to him, so he slipped quickly past the doorway to the next flight of stairs. These were really steep and narrow and had some slippery stuff on them instead of carpet. Except for a rather dim light on the landing, it was dark and completely quiet. For some reason this frightened him, and he felt that whatever was up there would not be like the other floors. It was a real test of courage and enterprise. He waited until he had got his breath back and then went for it. His feet made a clicking noise on the slippery stuff, and each step was higher than any he had climbed so far, and he got slower and slower as his heart thumped more and more loudly.

At length he could see a narrow door with a pointed top and a row of round holes near the bottom. He chose one and jumped through.

The room he found himself in was very large and there was very little light.

The windows – there was a second at the back – were indeed small and the glass encrusted with spiders' webs. It was also extremely full of furniture, or at least very large objects that seemed in the main to be broken: a table with one leg missing, various wrecked chairs, a huge cracked mirror, several heavy leather suitcases – mostly open and bulging with clothes and papers. Rolls of wallpaper, piles of cracked and broken plates, pot and pans dented or with holes in them, a sewing machine and an old gramophone with an enormous horn, funny sticks with a fat end that had once been filled in by a mesh but now had a large hole in the middle – he did not know what many of the objects were for – and everything was covered with dust. He scurried about looking at things, and after a bit he discovered that perhaps he was looking for something. Almost the moment he realised this, he found it.

Sitting on the floor beneath one of the dirty windows was an amazing house. It was red brick with a slate roof and a scarlet front door with windows each side of it. It had two floors, and the ones above had curtains. The red front door had a knocker on it – a lion's head with the ring knocker in his mouth. He thought he would see if he could look inside through one of the windows. By standing on his hind legs and putting his front paws on the windowsill, he could. In spite of the dusky light he could see a beautiful room with walls papered in green and white stripes, and tiny little pictures of people in gold frames stuck on them. And the furniture! There was a sofa, and two gilded chairs, several small tables – one with a bowl of flowers on it, one with a tea tray. Over the fireplace was a mirror divided into three parts, its frame gold with fruit and flowers carved at the top. There was a carpet embroidered with roses, and hanging from the centre of the ceiling a marvellous thing with tiny candles. Then he noticed in one corner of the room someone was lying on their back with their arms spread out. Were they asleep? He watched to see if they would wake up and see him, but they did not move. *Brave . . . enterprising . . .* echoed in his head. He went back to the front door and pushed it. It gave way, and he was in. He was in the hallway; there was a doorway on the left to a room that was clearly where the inhabitants ate their meals; a long table with chairs on each side. The table had plates of delicious-looking food on it; jelly, fruit and a very large dish that contained a whole, long pink fish. He sprang onto the table, his mouth watering, but the food was not food at all – it was pretending to be food. He jumped off the table to see if there were any real crumbs on the carpet, but there was nothing – not a single crumb.

Back in the hall there was a staircase, but it was so small that he could easily run up it. Here were several rooms with beds in them, and in one he found another small person. She had long golden hair spread over the pillow and her eyes were open. He got onto her bed and sniffed her carefully. She did not move. She was a pretending person – like the food.

Sitting on her bed, the thought came to him that this was a mouse-sized house; he could live in it; become a serious mouseholder, raise a family in it. There were two drawbacks. The first was that he had nobody to raise a family with, and the second that going up and down all those endless frightening stairs without anyone seeing him was going to be very difficult.

He left the little house and went to one of the windows and looked out. Even when he scrabbled some of the cobwebs off one of the small panes of glass, it was too dark now to see anything clearly. He decided to go home.

Going down the flights of stairs was not quite so frightening as coming up them had been. The people at the bottom of the first were still listening to the box where there seemed to be some sort of fight going on: loud bangs and people screaming, but they were so occupied by it that it was easy to slip past them.

The next flight down was also easy. The music was now very quiet and there was a strong smell of cooking. He resisted a lonely chip that was sitting on the landing carpet and started on the last flight. Here he was stopped in his tracks by a truly terrifying sight.

The enormous old cat was crouched upon the bottom stair. She had her back to him, but her copious fur overflowed on each side until it nearly filled the stair. Even if she was asleep, she would smell him if he tried to pass her. Terrible tales his mother had told him about how cats tortured their victims – pretending to let them escape and then pouncing on them again and again – flooded his mind and for minutes he was unable to move, was frozen by fear. *Brave . . . enterprising* – that was what the toad had said to him, and so far he had been those things. He couldn't stop now.

So very quietly, carefully, he crept down the stairs; the cat remained motionless. Then, when he was only three steps behind the monster, he took a deep breath and murmuring 'Freddie forever!' he sprang onto the cat's back – almost on its head and off again – for a lightning dash to the gap under the front door, down the front steps and into the front garden. His heart was beating like a bird in a cage trying to get out. Then he realised that any minute someone might open the front door and the cat would be out and after him. So he hurried back to No. 16, Skirting Board West.

The home had been much enlarged during his absence, although it did not at first seem so as troops of mice were returning from the evening's hunt for food, and his mother was telling them where to put everything. It took him a few minutes to get accustomed to the dusky gloom (the roof was dimly lit by a generous gap between floorboards above and every evening Mrs Whitemouse made the older mice stuff it with shreds of coconut matting before everyone settled down for the night). She didn't notice Freddie at first until he touched noses with her.

'What a surprise! And where have you been, if it's not too much to ask?'

'Finding things out,' he replied. He suddenly realised how extremely tired he was, and how much he had been banking on an affectionate welcome. For a moment he was wracked with longing for Alphonse and Poppy and for him being Charley. But then he remembered that they were all happy together and that he was determined to be a successful mouse. 'I'm very glad to be home,' he offered, 'and I shan't be going away any more.'

The younger mice now realised that their hero had returned and clustered around him. 'Tell us a story, Freddie – please tell us an eNORmouse story!'

'Not tonight, no, really not tonight.'

To his surprise, his mother supported him. 'You leave him alone now, or you won't get any supper. Come over here, Freddie, and keep an eye on the little ones.' So he crouched by the Hat where five little pink noses were pointed upwards and a minute squeaking conveyed their hunger.

Eventually there was the silence that meant everyone was nibbling, and Mrs Whitemouse returned to the Hat dragging a long strip of ham that was mostly fat. 'Half for all of you, and half for me,' she said. She nibbled off a piece of outside rind and put it in the Hat, whereupon all the pink noses pointed at once to the middle of the nest and a most satisfactory skirmish ensued.

'Poor little Lavinia's aunt has died. You'd think she would be relieved, but not she! Cried her eyes out, she did, comes every afternoon to tell me what a good mouse her aunt really was – says it was only the accident that turned her difficult.'

A picture of Lavinia in the kitchen, being bullied by bossy Horatio, came to him; and then when Freddie had rescued her, her bright trustful eyes, her lovely translucent ears that blushed a darker pink when he looked at her, and her tiny delicate feet kept so charmingly clean, her glossy fur that was the grey of all good mice but somehow seemed to him a grey like no other. And she was alone – a state unsuitable for any mouse . . .

'I'll go and visit her tomorrow,' he said as casually as possible.

His mother darted a quick look at him. But, 'Do, dear,' was all she said.

Soon all the food was finished and everybody settled down to sleep.

But Freddie could not sleep. He tried counting ants in his mind; he went over and over again his last terrific bravery in jumping onto the horrible, dangerous cat's back; he imagined living grandly in the doll's house; smashing one small pane of glass and discovering an outside route to the attic; he went over his last meeting with the sorcerer toad and wished he had expressed his gratitude for all that most respected creature had taught him ... It was no good. He simply could not sleep a wink.

Eventually he gave up trying and crept very quietly around all his sleeping relations before running to the passage that led to the kitchen. There was a junction in it that led to the den where Lavinia had lived with her aunt.

All the while he was running, he did not think at all of what he would do when he got there. He simply knew that he must see her. Now – outside the passage to her house, he paused. What could he say? He should have brought an offering – some food. He could have chewed a daisy off the

Hat and laid it at her feet. But he had nothing. The passage was not straight, but wound around several corners. When he could dimly see that he was nearly there, he called her name. There was no answer, but he became aware of a strange sound – a low subdued sobbing.

He entered the den. It was quite small. There was one large bed – empty. But in the opposite corner were some bits of hay and paper. Lavinia lay on her side, her face buried in the hay, and she was crying so much it was no wonder she had not heard him.

'Lavinia,' he said gently.

She uttered a small shriek of terror and turned to face him. 'Go away! I told you never to come here! I'll – I'll get Freddie to come and fight you!'

'I am Freddie. There's no one else here. You're safe with me.'

When she seemed calmer, he said, 'Was it Horatio you were frightened of?'

She nodded. Two last tears dripped down her

face, but her eyes were fixed on his – as bright and trusting as he had remembered them.

'Well, he's never going to bother you again.'

'Would you mind awfully staying until it's morning?'

'I wouldn't mind at all.'

The translucent part of her ears turned a deep pink.

'Oh, thank you, Freddie! Thank you so much. You could have my aunt's bed.'

'I'd rather stay here – with you.' She had been trying to tidy her face and he put his nose against hers: she smelled deliciously of salt and fresh breadcrumbs and she kept quite still while he licked her sodden fur dry. 'In fact, I want to stay with you forever. If you agree?'

Without saying a word, she threw herself into his arms.

And so began their life together. Gradually he told her all about his adventures and what he had learned from them. He told her about the grand house on the top floor, about not wanting to be a mouse, and the sorcerer; he told her about being a tiger and the jungle, about being a dog and Poppy and Alphonse, and finally about his decision that it was much better to be a mouse. Which it was; it most certainly was. And Lavinia, who had listened with rapt attention, naturally agreed with him. 'But then, you are no ordinary mouse,' she said, and although he said of course he was, he didn't actually feel ordinary at all. I do hope you agree with him.

The End